SOUL POWER

SOUL POWER

By Tracey West

Based on the teleplays
"Blast From the Past" by Adam Beechen
and John Semper Jr.
and
"Static in Africa" by Dwayne McDuffie

SCHOLASTIC INC.
New York   Toronto   London   Auckland   Sydney
Mexico City   New Delhi   Hong Kong   Buenos Aires

ISBN 0-439-65622-2

12 11 10 9 8 7 6 5 4 3 2 1   4 5 6 7 8 9/0

Printed in the U.S.A.   40
First printing, September 2004

SOUL POWER

What's Up With Virgil?

Virgil Hawkins used to be just like everybody else. He went to school, hung out with his buddy, Richie, got yelled at by his dad, and got into fights with his big sister.

Then one day Virgil found himself in the wrong place at the wrong time. He got caught in a chemical explosion. A Big Bang. Everyone hit by the chemical ended up changing — in a big way. They became more than human. That's why they're called meta-humans. Each meta-human ended up with a different power.

After the Big Bang, Virgil found out he could

control static electricity. He can light up a whole city block with one energy blast. He can make metal bend, twist, or fly through the air.

Each meta-human has a different power. Unfortunately, most meta-humans decide to use their powers to cause trouble. But not Virgil. He decided to use his powers to become a super hero instead.

Richie helped him out. He hooked Virgil up with super hero gear like cool threads, and a metal disk that Virgil can use to surf the sky.

That's how Virgil became the super hero called Static. Get ready to watch him in action. It'll be a real shock to your system!

CHAPTER ONE
Old School

It was a sunny Saturday afternoon in Dakota City. Normally, Virgil Hawkins would be hanging with his friend, Richie, playing video games or eating chili fries at the mall. But not today.

Virgil's older sister, Sharon, volunteered at the Dakota Retirement Home. She had asked Virgil to come help her out. It had sounded like a good idea — at first. Then Sharon had introduced him to Morris Grant.

Morris was a skinny old man who always wore blue pajamas and a white bathrobe. What was left of his hair was pure white. Sharon had asked

Virgil to talk to Morris and keep him company. That didn't seem too hard.

But all Morris wanted to do was talk about the "good old days." And he kept asking Virgil to read from this goofy comic book, *Soul Power*. The beat-up cover showed an African-American super hero with an Afro, a gold medal around his neck, a green mask, and a red polyester shirt with a wide collar and lightning bolts on the sleeves. That was Soul Power. He was fighting a man wearing a giant hat.

Virgil sighed and turned the page. "'This was the final showdown,'" he read. "'Good versus evil. Soul Power braced himself. Would his superpowers stand up to . . . the horrible hats of the Haberdasher?'"

Virgil laughed. "Dig that! Soul Power's scared of hats!" This was the lamest comic book he had ever read.

Morris frowned. "Boy, don't be dissin' Soul Power! Those hats are deadly!"

"Come on, Mr. Grant," Virgil said. "How dangerous can a hat be?"

A gray-haired man sitting nearby piped up.

"Oh, leave the boy alone, Morris," he said, speaking with a British accent, "and stop interrupting. I keep hoping this time that arrogant Soul Power gets it in the chops."

Morris turned to the man and shook his fist. "Dennis, I'm this close to giving you a knuckle sandwich," he said, annoyed. He turned back to Virgil. "Just keep reading, Sparky."

Virgil hesitated. Why had Mr. Grant called him "Sparky"?

"And give it some groove," Morris continued. "You kids have no sense of style. Back in my day . . ."

Dennis groaned. "Not again."

Virgil felt the same way. Mr. Grant sounded like a broken record with all his stories about the past.

But Morris ignored them. "Back in my day, cars were faster, threads were finer, and the girls were foxy!"

Virgil couldn't take it anymore. He quickly looked at his watch, then rose from his chair. "That's it! Lunch break!"

"Hey!" Morris cried. "You're not done with *Soul Power*."

"Trust me," Virgil replied. "I'm *done* with *Soul Power*."

Virgil left the room. He had to find Sharon. He wasn't cut out for this. Dealing with old people was just not his thing.

He found his sister in the TV lounge. Several residents of the home were gathered around, watching a game show.

"Sharon, you've got to let me go home — please!" he pleaded.

Sharon spun around, her black ponytails bobbing. "What's wrong *now*?" she asked.

"It's Mr. Grant!" Virgil said. "He's making me crazy!"

Sharon shook her head. "Virgil, you said you'd come here to the retirement home and help me. Now you want to leave me shorthanded. What kind of help is that?"

"But . . ."

"This is community service, Virgil," Sharon continued. "It's your duty as a citizen. Besides, you could learn a few things from the older generation."

As Sharon walked away, Virgil called after her, frustrated. "Like what? How to annoy people?"

Virgil was about to follow her when he noticed a news bulletin flash across the TV set.

"We interrupt this broadcast for a special report," said the news reporter. "A major crime is in progress at the Dakota Museum of Technology. It began just moments ago."

The news camera showed the museum, a distinguished, old, brick building. Then a section of the building exploded, sending bricks flying! But that wasn't all.

Three tall, metal robots stomped toward the huge hole that had been blown into the building. Virgil had never seen anything like the robots before. They looked like something from a sci-fi movie.

"Uh-oh," Virgil said. "Looks like it's time for *my* kind of community service!"

He rushed out of the TV lounge, right past Mr. Grant, who had come looking for him.

"Whoa, slow down, boy! Where's the fire?" Morris asked.

Virgil didn't answer him. He ran up the stairs to the roof of the building and quickly changed into his Static gear — a blue shirt, blue pants, blue boots, and a blue and yellow cape. He was about to put on his mask when he heard a voice behind him.

"Static!"

Virgil turned around. It was Mr. Grant! What was he doing up here? And he knew Virgil's secret! Nobody else knew it, except for Richie.

"Uh, I guess you're wondering what's with the costume," Virgil said quickly, trying to think of a way to throw off Mr. Grant. "Well, I, uh . . ."

Morris stepped toward him. "Don't sweat it, boy," he said. "I knew you were Static when I first met you!"

Morris swept his right hand over Static's head. Sparks of electricity sizzled from his fingers. "Yep. I can feel the electrical field around you," Morris said.

Virgil was stunned. "How'd you do that?"

The older man grinned. "Because I have a secret identity, too. This'll help you recognize me."

Morris reached into his robe and pulled out a green mask. He wrapped it around his eyes.

"You're the Lone Ranger?" Virgil asked.

Morris struck a super hero pose. "No, boy. It's me . . . Soul Power!"

CHAPTER TWO
Professor Menace

Virgil blinked. This skinny old man was Soul Power? The Afro was long gone, but as Virgil looked, he realized Mr. Grant had the same face as the hero in the comic book.

"That's right, I'm Soul Power," Morris said. "And you're going to take me with you to that museum — quickly!"

"Why would I want to do a thing like that?" Virgil asked.

Morris stepped closer to Virgil. "Because if you don't, I'll tell all my friends I met a real super hero today . . . Virgil Hawkins!"

Virgil couldn't believe it. Would Mr. Grant really give up his secret identity? The old man looked serious. Still . . .

"No way!" Virgil said firmly. "You can't blackmail me! You're not going, and that's final!"

Seconds later, Static was soaring over Dakota City on his metal flying disk. He kept it airborne by constantly charging it with electric energy.

Next to him, Soul Power flew on an electrically charged manhole cover. Mr. Grant had won after all, and Static wasn't happy about it one bit. Soul Power looked silly in his old costume, which drooped now that Mr. Grant didn't have bulging muscles anymore, and he wobbled on his manhole cover.

"Are you sure you won't fall?" Static called to him.

"'Course not," Soul Power said, trying to steady himself. "Heck, in *my* day, I got around by surfing the power lines."

"They had *electricity* in your day?" Static joked.

"Don't be flip, Sparky," Soul Power warned.

"Please don't call me Sparky," Static replied. "How'd you get to be a super hero anyway?"

"Well, back in the day," Soul Power began, "I was just a normal cat, until I got in the way of some thugs who wanted to trash Hoover Dam. A transformer blew, giving me the power of ten turbines!"

So that explains it, Static thought. The electric transformer had supercharged Mr. Grant with electric energy.

"I fought all sorts of bad guys in my day," Soul Power continued. "But the worst of them all was my archenemy, Professor Menace!"

Static zoomed past a skyscraper and let out a laugh. "Professor Menace? What, was the name 'Doctor Bad Dude' already taken?"

"Laugh all you want kid," Soul Power said, his voice grave. "Menace came *this* close to taking over the world. I stopped him, but before I could capture him, he suddenly stepped back, hit a switch, and his whole lab exploded! I got out okay, but I never did find any trace of him."

To Static, the whole story sounded like something out of that goofy comic book. "A bad guy who wants to rule the world. That's original. Did he do it all by himself, or did he have help?"

"He used robots — *exactly* like the ones at the museum," Soul Power said.

That got Static's attention. "What?"

"That's why I had to come with you," Soul Power said. "Those robots on TV once belonged to Professor Menace."

Suddenly, Soul Power let out a cry. "Right on!" He jumped off his manhole cover onto some thick power lines. He electrified them, skimming along them like a surfer riding a wave.

"Hey, come back here!" Static cried. He sped up.

Seconds later, the Dakota Museum of Technology came into view below them. Three robots stomped out of the museum. Soul Power skidded to a stop, still floating on the power lines. Static hovered next to him.

Soul Power nodded. "Those are them, all right."

Static built up an electric charge in his hands. "Looks like about five minutes of work. Be right back!"

"No, wait!" Soul Power cried. But Static had already zoomed down toward the robots. He aimed a powerful electromagnetic blast right at them.

The blast sizzled the robots. But then something strange happened. The robots repelled the charge! A huge stream of electricity shot out of the chest of one of the robots. The charge slammed Static, knocking him off of his flying disk!

Before Static could hit the ground, Soul Power aimed a cloud of electricity underneath him. The electric cloud supported Static, and he landed slowly and safely on the sidewalk.

Soul Power raced up to him. "You kids today just don't listen, do you?" he scolded Static. "I just told you Professor Menace was my arch-enemy. That means he knows how to fight someone with electrical powers!"

Soul Power was right — and Static hated that. "Okay, so maybe I can't fire right at these old-school junk piles. But I have other tricks up my sleeve!"

Static sent another electric blast at the robots — but this time, he aimed it at their feet. It ripped through the pavement, breaking a hole in the ground. Two of the robots crashed down into the sewer.

Static grinned. He spotted an empty taxi parked nearby and zapped it with an electric charge. He sent it slamming into the third robot.

A fourth robot stomped out of the museum. Static acted quickly. He charged a street lamp, pulling it out of the ground and sending it zipping toward the robot. It wrapped around the robot like a snake, pinning it down.

Static turned to Soul Power. That old-timer would have to be impressed now!

"See? These oversized wind-up toys might have been da bomb back in your day, but —"

"Look out!" Soul Power cried, pointing behind Static. Before he could react, a huge mechanical hand swooped down from the sky and gripped him tightly. Static then found himself face-to-face with a giant silver robot. It had a round head, a huge round chest, and arms and legs like tree trunks.

Suddenly, Static felt his whole body tingle. He could see glowing electricity start to flow from his body. He felt weaker and weaker with each second.

"He's draining you!" Soul Power cried.

Static felt like he had no energy to break free.

Back on the ground, Soul Power raised his fist in the air. "After all these years, it's time for a little Soul Power!" the hero cried.

Glowing green electricity poured down from the sky. It encircled Soul Power, charging his body with an incredible amount of power. He zapped a nearby manhole cover and flew up to the giant robot.

Wham! Wham! He smashed the robot's face with his electrified fist. The robot loosened its grip, and Static fell to the ground. Soul Power flew down to his side.

Static opened his eyes — in time to see the robot's massive foot about to stomp them both! But Soul Power had it covered.

"Back off!" he cried, raising both his arms. He created an electric force field that slammed into the robot's foot, sending the huge creation tumbling backward.

Soul Power approached the fallen robot. "Menace, I know you're listening!" he called out. "It's me, Soul Power!"

A panel in the robot's chest slid open. A black-and-white picture of a man in a mask appeared on the screen. It looked exactly like Professor Menace — thirty years ago!

Soul Power looked surprised. "How can you still be so young?"

Professor Menace chuckled. "When I destroyed my lab, I slipped into a secret chamber, where I was frozen and preserved!"

The robot slowly rose to its feet. A tray slid out from its chest, revealing old vacuum tubes and transistors.

"Now I've reawakened in this modern time," he said, "and I can finish what I started years ago!"

"Well, I'm not going to let you get away with this!" Soul Power yelled. He lunged forward.

Static tried to get up, but he was still too weak to fight. In the next instant, red beams shot out of the robot's eyes. They slammed into Soul Power, and he collapsed next to Static.

Professor Menace grinned. "Alas, dear Soul Power, you just don't have the juice. How fitting that I should be the one to finally put out your lights!"

Static and Soul Power watched, helpless, as the giant robot leaned down and scooped them up with its electricity-sucking hand.

CHAPTER THREE
The Power Pad

Static raised his head. He was still weak from the robot's last attack, but he had a little energy left. Not enough to take down the robot — but enough to make something happen!

Next to the robot stood a large construction crane with a demolition ball hanging from it. Static knew just what to do. Taking a deep breath, he zapped the metal cable attached to the ball. The solid metal ball swung at the robot, slamming it in the chest.

Wham! The mighty blow sent the robot falling

backward. It loosened its grip on Soul Power and Static, and they crashed to the ground.

Static rose to his feet and helped Soul Power get up. The robot was down, but not out. It stood up and stomped toward them. Then it suddenly stopped. Professor Menace's face appeared on the screen once again.

"I could destroy you now, but I'll wait," he said. "I want you to participate in my ultimate moment of triumph."

The top of the robot's head opened, and a large propeller rose up. As the propeller spun around, orange flames shot out of the robot's hands. Then it lifted into the air like a rocket and flew away.

Static shook his head. "That robot took us out like we were nothing," he said.

"We're not licked yet, Sparky," Soul Power replied.

Static had had enough. "Will you *stop* calling me that? And from now on, there's no more 'we.' If I'm gonna get whooped again, I don't need your commentary!"

Static zapped his flying disk, hopped on it, and

flew away without looking back. He hated being taken down by a bunch of tin cans. *That old man cramped my style,* Static told himself as he zipped across town. *I gotta do my own thing — my own way.*

When Virgil changed out of his gear and got home, he found his dad sitting in the living room. Robert Hawkins peered at Virgil through his glasses.

"What happened to you, Virgil?" he asked. "Sharon told me you left the retirement home early today."

Virgil tried to change the subject. "Hey, Pops, do you remember a super hero from the old days called Soul Power?"

Mr. Hawkins's eyes lit up. "Do I? Are you kidding? Soul Power was the greatest! Wait right here."

Virgil's dad went to the basement and came back a few minutes later with an old-fashioned film projector, a metal can of film, and a portable movie screen. He set up the screen, turned down the lights, threaded the film into the projector, and turned it on.

A grainy, black-and-white film flickered on the screen. Soul Power, complete with his Afro and polyester shirt, was chasing a gang of thugs in suits. He slammed one with an electric punch. Then he blasted two, sending them slamming into a brick building. A fourth one ran away, but Soul Power created a round jail cell from electric energy. He sent the electric cell flying on top of the criminal, trapping him. Then he did a groovy victory dance, shaking his hips and waving his arms.

Virgil's dad was loving every minute of it. He danced along with Soul Power, flapping his elbows like some kind of demented chicken.

"Pops, do *not* dance!" Virgil begged.

Mr. Hawkins chuckled and switched off the projector. "Soul Power was a real hero, all right. I had all his comic books . . . until my mother made me throw them away. Oh, the money I could have made!"

"Yo, I just asked what you knew about him. I didn't realize you were a superfan," Virgil said, a bit annoyed. His pops never got this excited about Static.

"People forget that he was the Static of his day," Mr. Hawkins replied. "Maybe even better."

Virgil gasped. "I don't think so!"

Just then, the doorbell rang. Virgil jumped up to get it. Anything was better than listening to his pops drool over that lame super hero. But Sharon came out of the kitchen and beat him to the door. When she opened it, Morris Grant stood there. He wore a brown suit, a trench coat, and a porkpie hat.

"Hello, Missy," he said, smiling.

Sharon smiled back. "Mr. Grant! What brings you here?"

"Virgil promised to help me with something . . . if he's not too busy."

Mr. Hawkins stepped up behind Virgil and nudged him forward. "Of course. He's not busy at all."

Virgil panicked. He was *not* going to get roped into crime fighting with this old-timer again. "Are you kidding? I've got to clean my room, mow the lawn, and have you *seen* our gutters lately?"

"Virgil, if you made a promise, you'd better keep it," Sharon said sternly.

Virgil sighed. There was no way around it. "All right, all right."

Minutes later, Soul Power and Static were surfing the power lines of Dakota City.

"I have a plan. I know how we can find out what Professor Menace is up to," Soul Power said. "Just follow me."

"Fine," Static said. He might as well do what the old guy wanted. He wasn't easy to get rid of. Sailing along the power lines cheered him up a little, though.

"Actually, this is pretty cool," Static admitted.

Soul Power looked over his shoulder and smirked. "It beats riding the senior shuttle bus!"

Soul Power eventually jumped down from the power lines and landed in front of an abandoned subway station. Static followed him down the dark and dirty stairway.

"So this is your big plan? To hide in this smelly old station?" Static asked.

Soul Power didn't answer right away. He walked up to a metal door secured with a combination lock. He put his hand on the lock, charged it, and it fell open. The door creaked loudly as Soul Power pushed it open.

"My plan begins inside here."

The door led to a dark, narrow tunnel. Soul Power stepped inside. Static shook his head and walked behind him.

"Welcome, Sparky, to my old headquarters, the Power Pad!" Soul Power said proudly.

Static wasn't impressed. "I mean it! Stop calling me —"

Soul Power stopped and turned on the lights with a quick jolt of electricity. Static gasped. The tunnel led to a huge, circular room loaded with old computers, gadgets, monitors, and other strange-looking mechanical equipment. A silver disco ball hung in the center.

"Whoa! You have *got* to be kidding!" Static said, impressed.

Soul Power headed to one of the machines, a metal box topped with glass globes. Soul Power put his palm over one of the globes and gave it a charge. The globe hummed and glowed. Then a chain reaction started, and soon all of the machines in the room were lit up and humming.

"This place is cool. Why'd you give it a lame name like the 'Power Pad'?" Static asked.

"Hey, it was cool in my time," Soul Power said. "Why? Where do *you* hang out?"

"Uh, the Abandoned Gas Station of Solitude," Static answered meekly. He had to admit it sounded kind of silly.

Static looked around while Soul Power fiddled with a giant computer. It was the size of four refrigerators put together. A row of round reels lined the front of the computer, along with an array of buttons and slots.

On a table near the computer, Static saw a black-and-white photo in a frame. He picked it up. It showed Soul Power standing next to a younger super hero wearing a skintight costume and a face mask.

"Who's that?" Static asked.

Soul Power glanced back at the photo. "That was my teenage sidekick, Sparky."

Soul Power turned back to the computer. Static looked up and grinned. Suddenly the nickname Sparky didn't seem so bad.

Soon Soul Power had the computer reels whirring. He pressed some buttons on the keyboard. A few seconds later, a long strip of paper shot out of a slot. Soul Power read it and frowned.

"I was afraid of this," he said. He walked across the room and turned on a large television monitor. He pressed another button, and a black-and-white video began to play.

A peaceful-looking town appeared on the screen. Then, suddenly, dark clouds filled the sky. Lightning and rain hammered the town. A whirling tornado came out of nowhere, knocking down buildings.

Soul Power narrated the tape. "Seaside, Georgia. Peaceful little place, until Menace came to visit with a lean, mean weather machine!"

Soul Power turned off the screen. "The computer says he's at the weather control game again. That's why he stole all that equipment from the museum. And if we don't stop him —"

"He'll rule the world! Nyah-ha-ha!" Static joked, doing his best impersonation of an evil villain.

But Soul Power looked grave. "Right on."

"So how do we stop him?"

Soul Power opened a metal case. He pulled out a metal gadget that looked something like a walkie-talkie.

"This is an electro-amplifier," he said. "It can briefly boost your power in an emergency."

Static warily examined the gadget. "Or, since it's over thirty years old, it could short out and fry me."

Soul Power nodded. "Good point. Better use it as a last resort."

Static added it to his gear anyway. "I hope this isn't why Sparky's not around anymore," he muttered.

He followed Soul Power to the back of the room to a massive shape covered by a tarp.

"We're ready to go. But we're going in style," Soul Power said. "I give you . . . the Soulmobile!"

Soul Power whipped off the tarp to reveal a bulky gray car with tail fins. The yellow *Soul Power* logo was painted on the hood.

Static made a face. The Soulmobile looked like a hunk of junk, but what choice did he have? Soul

Power climbed in the driver's seat, and Static hopped in next to him.

Soul Power pressed a button, and a panel slid open on the wall, revealing a long, dark tunnel. He revved up the engine.

"Hang on, Sparky!" Soul Power cried. "We've got a villain to catch!"

CHAPTER FOUR
In the Clutches of Professor Menace

The Soulmobile tore through the tunnel and emerged into the daylight, driving through the outskirts of town, toward Dakota City.

"Where are we going?" Static shouted, as the wind whipped through his dreads.

"To see a man about a map," Soul Power shouted back. "A weather map."

Soul Power drove downtown and parked in front of a tall, gleaming skyscraper. The sign out front read, TRANSGLOBAL SATELLITE. Men and women in business suits stopped and stared as Static and Soul Power got out of the car and headed for the elevators. Soul Power pressed the button for the penthouse.

The elevator doors opened to a fancy lobby. A secretary sat behind a large, glass desk. She nodded at them.

"Mr. Rollins heard about your arrival," she said. "Go right in."

She pointed to an office door, and Static followed Soul Power inside. A man with graying hair and glasses sat behind a desk. Behind him, large windows showed a spectacular view of Dakota City.

Mr. Rollins shook his head. "After all these years, I can't believe it."

"Believe it, Phil," Soul Power said. "I'm back and I need your help. I want access to your satellites."

Of course, Static realized. *If Professor Menace was planning to mess with the weather, a worldwide satellite system could tell them what he was up to.*

"I'm sorry, Soul Power," Mr. Rollins said. "I can't allow that unless you're a government-approved client."

"Look," Soul Power pleaded. "Years ago, you were a young man who used to call me his idol. Now you're the head of this big satellite firm. Don't tell me you're too high-and-mighty to help an old friend!"

Phil sighed. "Times have changed, Soul Power. Everything these days is about clearance. I can't do it." He pulled a white security card out of his pocket and waved it to make his point. Then he set it on the desk in front of him.

Soul Power leaned forward. "Back in the day, I fought so that young men like you would have a chance to get to this position."

"You also taught us not to break rules," Mr. Rollins pointed out. "And I won't, not even for you. Besides, aren't you too old for this sort of thing?"

Soul Power pounded his fist on the desk. "You're never too old to fight for justice!"

"I'm not so sure about that," Static muttered.

"I'm sorry, Soul Power," Mr. Rollins said sadly.

Soul Power turned and walked away. "Come on, kid," he told Static, "we have work to do."

"Is he the new Sparky?" Mr. Rollins asked.

"No!" Static said firmly, shutting the door behind him.

They went back to the Soulmobile and zoomed down the street.

"Now what?" Static asked.

"Back to the Power Pad. I need to tap into those top-secret satellites." Soul Power grinned and held up the white security card. "You know, things stick to you when you have static electricity!"

"Right on!" Static said.

Back at the Power Pad, Soul Power fed the security card into his computer. The large screen on the wall lit up, showing a satellite map of Earth.

"Solid! Now search for any kind of rare weather pattern," Soul Power instructed.

Static operated the keyboard, scanning the satellite map. Most of it looked normal. Then the screen zoomed in on North America. A small area blinked red.

"Uh-oh," Static said. He zoomed closer.

Soul Power frowned. "It's outside Dakota City, in the high hills."

They ran out of the Power Pad. Static hopped on

his flying disk, and Soul Power charged up another manhole cover. They flew toward the hills on the outskirts of town.

"I think I'm finally getting the hang of this," Soul Power said. Even Static had to admit he looked much steadier than before.

Soon they came to the hills. "What exactly are we looking for?" Static asked.

Before Soul Power could answer, a flurry of wind and snow hit them, almost knocking them down. It was a blizzard — in the middle of summer!

"Never mind," Static said.

They flew through the snow. Suddenly, Soul Power pointed down at the hills. Static looked down and saw a large concrete building, topped by a metal dome. A long rod extended from the dome.

"It's got to be his headquarters," Soul Power said. "That's his weather machine on the top."

Soul Power began to drop toward the ground. "Remember, this time we work as a team," he told Static.

The two heroes landed in front of the large, arch-shaped doors at the front of the headquarters.

They turned to each other, nodded, then blasted open the doors. They zoomed in side by side.

They didn't get far. Two huge mechanical arms swept down from the ceiling, grabbing them tightly. As Static struggled to free himself, lights came on in the building. He saw what must be the base of the weather machine in front of them — a huge contraption with tubes snaking out of it and glass bubbles sticking out from the sides. Then a large screen slid down from the ceiling in front of them.

The face of Professor Menace appeared on the screen. "How fortunate for me that you two dropped in," he said smugly. "And just in time."

"What do you mean?" Soul Power asked.

Professor Menace grinned. "I was missing one component for my weather machine — enough power to make it truly effective. Now you two shall be my batteries!"

In the next instant, Static felt his whole body shake as the metal arm began to drain the electricity from him. A force field of white electric energy surrounded him. He could see the same thing happening to Soul Power in the other arm.

Static couldn't break free. He watched, helpless, as the stolen energy flowed through the arms and into the weather machine. The tubes and glass bubbles began to glow and crackle with the charge.

Professor Menace cackled. "When the world sees what I do to Dakota City, they'll pay me to never do it again!"

CHAPTER FIVE
Sparky!

Static and Soul Power writhed as the mechanical arms continued to drain their power, feeding the huge weather machine.

"All . . . my . . . fault!" Soul Power struggled to get out the words. "This was . . . a trap!"

Static tried to think. There had to be *something* they could do.

Then he remembered the electro-amplifier from the Power Pad. If he could just reach it! Static used his last bit of power to zap the electro-amplifier from his belt into his hand.

"Maybe I can use this to short-circuit the arm,"

he told Soul Power, slapping the gadget onto the metal.

There was a popping and sizzling sound as the electro-amplifier released a huge surge of power. Just as Static had hoped, it short-circuited the mechanical arm. The arm opened, sending Static tumbling to the floor.

Static grunted, then jumped to his feet. He ran to a nearby computer console and started pressing buttons. Slowly, the machine began to shut down. The other mechanical arm lowered, dropping Soul Power on the floor. He groaned as Static ran to his side.

"Soul Power! Are you okay?"

Static helped Soul Power to his feet. The older man looked shaken. "Maybe I *am* too old for this," he said weakly. "Thanks to me, Dakota City is doomed."

"But we turned off the weather machine," Static said.

"That won't stop Professor Menace," Soul Power said. "We've got to find him."

Static nodded. "We need to get back to the city."

"How?" Soul Power asked. "We don't have enough power left to fly. I can barely walk."

"Maybe I can help."

Static and Soul Power turned around as Phil Rollins stepped into the room.

"Mr. Rollins! What are you doing here?" Static asked.

"Menace has taken over my satellites," Rollins said. "He's using them to control the weather. I know where he is, but I can't stop him without your help."

"How'd you find us?" Static asked.

Mr. Rollins turned to Soul Power. He took a small silver box out of his pocket and grinned.

"I still have our old tracers — partner," he said.

Soul Power chuckled. "Just like old times, eh?"

Suddenly, the truth hit Static. "Whoa! You're Sparky?"

Mr. Rollins unbuttoned his shirt to reveal a blue costume with a yellow lightning bolt on the front.

"That's right," he replied. "My old costume stretches enough to still fit. You guys ready for a recharge?"

Soul Power thrust a fist into the air. Static and Sparky did the same.

"You bet!" Soul Power cried. "Get ready, world, 'cause it's time for a little —"

Sparky released a blast of electric energy. It surged through Soul Power and Static. A green ball of glowing electricity engulfed the three heroes. Together, they let out a mighty battle cry.

"SOOOOOOOOOOUL POWERRRRRRRRRR!"

CHAPTER SIX
Dennis the Menace

Static, Soul Power, and Sparky lifted up from the ground, surrounded by a green bubble of electric energy. They burst through the dome-shaped roof and sailed off toward Dakota City.

"So, how did you get your powers?" Static asked Sparky, as they flew over the treetops.

"My costume is electrically charged," Sparky explained. "I invented it when I was a kid, to be like him."

Sparky nodded toward Soul Power, and Static could see how much Sparky looked up to the older hero. He was starting to understand why. Soul

Power might have gray hair and like to talk about the old days a lot, but he was tough, smart, and never gave up.

As they neared Dakota City, Static could see the place was in a panic. Snow, sleet, and wind whipped through the streets. People ran for cover, confused. They had to find Professor Menace, and fast.

"So, where to, Sparky?" Soul Power asked.

"How should I know?" Static replied.

"He was talking to me," Sparky said. "Down there. In that building."

Static and Soul Power looked down.

"The Dakota Retirement Home?" Static was shocked. What was Professor Menace doing there?

Sparky nodded. "Yes. According to my data, he's somewhere underground."

They landed in front of the retirement home, walked inside, then headed to the basement. It was empty except for a large furnace and a sink. Sparky pointed toward a gray concrete wall.

"Blast through it!" he cried.

Static obeyed, slamming the wall with an electric charge. The wall crumbled, and the three heroes raced through the gaping hole.

They found themselves in a room crammed with whirring machines, a large screen, and a console. Professor Menace stood in front of the console wearing a long white lab coat, black gloves, black boots, and a pair of red goggles over his eyes. He whirled around.

"No! Not you again!" he cried.

Soul Power turned to Static and Sparky. "He's my enemy," he said firmly. "Leave him to me!"

Professor Menace turned to two metal robots leaning against the far wall. "Destroy them!" he ordered.

The robots came to life and charged toward Static and Sparky. Sparky aimed an electric charge at a nearby wall, sending a sheet of thick concrete crashing down on one of the robots. The other robot advanced on Static.

At the same time, Soul Power ran toward Professor Menace. Before he could get close, red beams shot out from the professor's goggles, knocking Soul Power across the room.

While Soul Power struggled to his feet, Sparky

finished off his robot. The robot tried to shake off the concrete sheet that was on top of him, but Sparky jumped up on it first. He reached down and twisted off the robot's metal head.

On the other side of the room, the second robot aimed powerful punches at Static, who zipped through the air, dodging each blow.

Soul Power lunged toward Professor Menace again. This time, he stretched his arms out in front of him, sending bolts of green electric energy shooting from his fingertips. Professor Menace fought back by blasting more red beams from his goggles. The two force fields met, but neither was strong enough to overpower the other.

Meanwhile, Static found a chance to take down his robot. He aimed a blast of electricity right at the robot's chest. Sparky ran up behind the robot and aimed another blast at his back. The two used the electric current to send the robot spinning up to the ceiling at superspeed. The sheer force of the movement caused the robot to break into pieces.

With the robots taken care of, Static and Sparky ran up behind Soul Power. He was assaulting Professor Menace with every ounce of power he had, but it just wasn't enough.

Static and Sparky looked at each other.

"You thinking what I'm thinking?" Static asked.

Sparky gave Static a high five. "Right on!"

The two turned back to Professor Menace and blasted power from their hands. The double jolt joined with Soul Power's energy blast.

Wham! The powerful charge slammed into Professor Menace, sending him clear across the room.

They ran to the fallen professor, who lay on his back with his eyes closed. As they watched, a strange rippling effect crossed the professor's face. When it stopped, the young face of Professor Menace had been replaced by a wrinkled face with gray hair!

"Look! It was a holographic illusion," Soul Power exclaimed. "He really is old, like me."

Static reached down and yanked off Professor Menace's red goggles. He gasped. He had seen that face before — in the retirement home! He had been in the room when Virgil was reading the comic book.

"Dennis!" Soul Power cried.

The unmasked villain sighed. "All these years I've waited and planned my revenge," he said wearily. "And now, you still won. I should've stuck to basket-weaving." Then he fainted and fell back to the floor.

It didn't take long for things to return to normal. They delivered Professor Menace to the police, and the snowstorm stopped. Static and Soul Power said good-bye to Sparky, then changed out of their costumes. Virgil followed Mr. Grant to his room in the retirement home.

"Well, that's that," Morris said, putting his green mask back in his dresser drawer. "With the last of my super-villains out of the way, Soul Power is officially retired."

Virgil realized that this made him sad. Fighting crime with Soul Power had actually been pretty cool. Virgil felt bad about giving the old guy such a hard time in the beginning.

"Listen," Virgil said, shyly, "I, uh, just wanted to say I, uh, learned a lot from you after all. So, you know, thanks."

Morris shrugged. "Hey, that's what you do with knowledge, kid. You pass it on."

Virgil still had unfinished business. He walked to the open door and made sure no one was watching.

"You know, there's one thing you didn't teach me," Virgil said.

"What's that?" Morris asked.

"It's that dance," Virgil said. "How do those funky moves go?"

Morris's eyes lit up. He moved to a cassette player on his dresser and pushed a button. Funky soul music began to play.

"First of all, you got to muster up a little . . . Soooooooul Powerrrrrr!" Morris cried. Then he began to boogie down.

Virgil tried to follow along, smiling. Sharon had been right — there was a lot to learn from the older generation.

"Right on!" Virgil said.

CHAPTER SEVEN
Static in Africa

Not long after Virgil's adventures with Soul Power and Professor Menace, the Hawkins family boarded a plane bound for Ghana, Africa.

It was a long flight. Virgil, Sharon, and Mr. Hawkins sat together in a row. Virgil kept busy reading a stack of super hero comic books. Sharon read fashion magazines, and Mr. Hawkins talked (and talked and talked) about Africa.

"Ah, Africa, the motherland, cradle of humanity!" Mr. Hawkins gushed. "We're almost there. Can you feel the electricity?"

Virgil rubbed his left arm. "I can't feel anything after the twenty-three shots I had to get."

"You took them all in your arm?" Sharon asked.

"You know where they wanted me to take them?" Virgil asked. His sister rolled her eyes.

Their dad turned the pages of an Africa tour book. "Your mother and I always dreamed of bringing you here," he said. "We saved for this trip since you were little."

Virgil had heard that story about a hundred times already — along with every other fact about Africa that his father could remember. He decided to tease his dad.

"I just want to see the tigers," Virgil said.

Mr. Hawkins frowned. "There aren't any —"

"Tigers in Africa," Virgil finished. "I know. I just said it to get your goat. Are there any goats?"

"Actually, there are thousands of species," Mr. Hawkins said. "Elephants, roan antelopes, lion hartebeests, leopard waterbucks, bongo chim-panzees, bushbuck olive baboons . . ."

Virgil and Sharon exchanged looks. Once Mr. Hawkins started, there was no stopping him. They put their headphones on at the same time and leaned back.

A few hours later, the plane landed. They collected their luggage and walked outside the airport into the African sunlight. People walked by, some in American-looking clothes, while others wore colorful African dresses. Cars and buses zipped by on the street in front of the airport, and Virgil could see tall buildings in the distance.

Mr. Hawkins beamed. "Oh, children, just look at it!"

"Yo, Pops, it's an airport," Virgil pointed out.

"Yes, but it's an airport in *Africa*," Mr. Hawkins said.

Virgil sighed. He was ready to see more of Africa than the airport. He let out a loud whistle. "Taxi!" he cried.

Sharon stepped next to him, shaking her head. She waved her hand in the air. "*Tro-tro!*" she called out.

"*Tro-tro?*" Virgil asked.

Sharon pointed to a boxy-looking minibus heading toward them. "That's what you call those vehicles," she said. "Some of us were paying attention when Daddy was telling us all the boring stuff."

The *Tro-tro* pulled up in front of them. The driver, a thin African man with a mustache, got out and helped them with their bags. They climbed on board with the other passengers, and the *Tro-tro* took off through Accra, the capital city of Ghana. The driver told them about the sights as they drove by.

"Accra has been the capital of Ghana for more than two hundred years," he explained. "Ours was the first black African colony to achieve independence."

"From the British, in 1957," Mr. Hawkins told Virgil and Sharon.

The *Tro-tro* drove past a huge monument — a stone archway topped by a black marble star. The engraving on top of the arch read: AD 1957. FREEDOM AND JUSTICE.

"What's that?" Virgil asked.

"Independence Monument," the driver replied. "The black star represents African freedom from colonialism."

Then the driver pointed to a long, brick building resting on green grass. "Over here is the W.E.B. DuBois Center, where the great American civil rights leader is buried."

"That's right," Sharon said. "He was a proponent of Pan-Africanism."

"Didn't we get a shot for that?" Virgil joked.

"Pan-Africanism is the belief of the unity of all black people and their cultural connection to Africa," his sister explained, her dark eyes shining. "It says that the blood and history we share bind us together as strong as any national border. One people, many lands. Can you feel it?"

Virgil looked out the window. Outside, people crowded a marketplace filled with stalls. There were some tourists, but most of the people were African. People who looked just like him. Virgil smiled. "Yeah," he said, "I feel it."

That night, Virgil lay awake in bed in the hotel room he shared with his dad. Across the room, his dad was snoring loudly, exhausted from the long trip. Virgil couldn't sleep. Tomorrow they would begin their tour of Africa, but Virgil couldn't wait — and he didn't have to. Quietly, he got out of bed and unzipped his suitcase.

Minutes later, Static was soaring across the night sky on his flying disk. He soared outside the city of Accra to the plains of Ghana. Stars glittered in the deep purple sky above him. Below, trees dotted the green landscape. Static swooped by a tall giraffe munching on a tree branch.

Static was feeling something big — and he wanted to share it with someone. He took out his ShockVox, a handheld communication device his friend Richie had invented so they could keep in contact with each other.

"Richie? Richie?" The ShockVox was silent.

"Right," Static realized. "Guess I'm a *little* out of range."

Static zapped the ShockVox with a burst of energy to give it extra juice. The gadget crackled and came to life.

"Richie? Are you there?" Static asked.

His best friend's voice answered him. "V-man! How's the trip?"

"It's amazing. There are black people everywhere," Static replied.

"Dude, you're in Africa," Richie pointed out.

Static smiled. He soared across the plains, passing a herd of elephants. "No, Richie," he said. "I mean, ever since I got here, I've felt different . . . connected." It was kind of hard to explain.

"You know, when my dad went to Ireland, he got all goofy, too," Richie said.

"It's not like that," Static said, searching for the right words. "It's like I've been carrying this weight around all my life without knowing it. And now it's gone."

"What are you talking about, Virg?"

"In Africa, I'm not a *black* kid. I'm just a kid. Is this what it feels like for you all the time?" Static asked.

There was a pause. Finally, Richie answered. "Yeah, I guess."

Static rose into the air. A huge, full moon brightened the night sky. He made a wide, joyous loop in front of the moon. Below him, cheetahs raced across the plains.

"Feels good!" Virgil cried.

CHAPTER EIGHT
Danger on the Train

Early the next morning, Virgil and his family headed for the Accra train station. They were on their way to their next stop — Kumasi. The ancient capital of the Ashanti tribe, Kumasi was the largest cultural center in West Africa.

Virgil's sister had jumped into the spirit of their trip. Instead of wearing her hair in pigtails, like she usually did, Sharon had wrapped it up in an orange scarf. She wore a yellow blouse, a blue and orange skirt, and sandals.

"Honey, you look so beautiful — like you really belong in Africa," Mr. Hawkins said, beaming.

"Yeah, maybe we should leave her here," Virgil cracked.

Sharon glowered at him, but before she could reply, the train pulled into the station. The Hawkins family climbed aboard and settled into their comfortable seats. The two wide seats faced each other with a table in the middle.

Virgil looked around the train. Just like at the airport, there was a mix of tourists — people in American-looking clothing and others in colorful African garb. One woman sitting in the corner wore a dark Moroccan robe. A scarf covered the bottom half of her face, and her eyes seemed to look through Virgil as they exchanged glances. Virgil shivered a little and took out a comic book to read.

A man with gray hair, glasses, and a beard walked up to their seats. He wore a white shirt, shorts, and carried a briefcase.

"Is this seat taken?" he asked, pointing to the empty seat across from Mr. Hawkins.

"Please," Virgil's dad said.

The two men shook hands. "I am Doctor Anokye,

professor of archaeology at the University of Ghana," the man said.

"I'm Robert Hawkins, and these are my children, Sharon and Virgil," Mr. Hawkins replied. "We're tourists."

Dr. Anokye's eyes had a friendly gleam. "From America, yes? Perhaps we are distant cousins. One never knows."

Mr. Hawkins nodded his head. "That's true, kids. About sixteen percent of all slaves came from Ghana."

"We gotta ditch Pop's books," Virgil whispered to his sister.

Mr. Hawkins and Dr. Anokye continued their conversation. "I want to show my kids where the Ashanti kings used to live," Virgil's dad was saying.

Suddenly, a loud *BAM!* rocked the train. The sound came from the roof.

Virgil looked up. A clawed hand was ripping through the ceiling of the train, creating a large, gaping hole! People on the train began to scream and run as a strange figure jumped through the hole.

Virgil gasped. The intruder was tall and power-fully built. His body was covered in pale yellow fur, and his face looked just like a leopard's. He had a long tail, claws on his hands and feet, and wore an orange vest.

"It's Osebo!" someone yelled. "Run for your lives!"

"This was not in the brochures!" Virgil joked nervously.

The leopard man headed right for Dr. Anokye. The elderly man clutched his briefcase to his chest.

"You can give me your briefcase," Osebo growled, leaning into the doctor's face. He bran-dished his left claw, which was made entirely of metal, "or I can tear it away. Your choice, doc-tor."

"Hey, Catman," Virgil said angrily. "Leave him alone!"

"I quite agree," said someone from behind him.

Virgil turned. The Moroccan woman was stand-ing in the aisle, her eyes locked on Osebo. But her voice had been low and deep, like a man's. Before Osebo could turn around, she aimed a powerful punch across his back. It sent Osebo sprawling across the railroad car. He jumped to his feet and gave an angry growl.

The Moroccan woman began to spin around, whirling like a tornado. In the next second, she had transformed into a tall man with a white mask over his face. He wore a black hat with a red spider emblazoned on it. His black cape, lined in red, bore the same red spider symbol on it. He carried a wood staff in his gloved hands. A black shirt, black pants, and tall gray boots rounded out his costume.

"I suggest we stand on tradition, Osebo," said the mysterious man. "You know the ancient story well. The spider always catches the leopard."

The spider man twirled his staff and faced Osebo, ready for battle.

"*Whoa!*" Virgil cried.

CHAPTER NINE
We're Going to Crash!

"What do you say, leopard friend?" asked the man in the spider costume. "Shall we dance?"

Osebo growled and swiped at the spider man, who jumped up, propelled himself off a seat, and flipped in the air over Osebo's head. He landed firmly on his feet on the opposite end of the train car.

Virgil was impressed. This was a genuine super hero — right here in Africa!

"Who is that?" Virgil asked.

"I am Anansi the Spider, ever at your service,"

the man said, giving a low bow. Then he turned his attention back to Osebo.

Osebo swiped at Anansi with his sharp claws once again. Anansi blocked the blow with his staff.

"He is the most famous crime fighter in all of West Africa!" Dr. Anokye said proudly.

"I was too modest to say," Anansi added, not taking his eyes from Osebo. He thrust his staff at Osebo, but the leopard man jumped, avoiding it. With his next motion, Osebo slammed into Anansi's chest, knocking the hero onto his back. Then he pounced!

Anansi was ready. He caught Osebo in midair, then pushed him backward with his feet. Osebo crashed onto the train floor, growling angrily.

Anansi rose to his feet first.

"Hit him with a web blast!" Virgil called out, thinking of another hero in a spider costume.

"I am not that kind of spider," Anansi said. He held out his hands, and a glowing white light appeared in front of him. "And this is not that kind of web!"

The glowing light took the shape of a large spiderweb, and settled over the train. Immediately, the floor of the train underneath Osebo seemed to vanish. Virgil could see the tracks as the train sped over them.

Osebo jumped up, grasping at the train ceiling with his claws. He hung there for a second, looking warily at the open floor beneath him. Anansi sat down in an empty seat and chuckled at Osebo's predicament.

Osebo cautiously lowered his foot to the floor, then shook his head.

"Always with your tricks!" The leopard man jumped down, and his feet firmly hit the train floor, which appeared once again.

It was an illusion, Virgil realized. It just *looked* like the train floor had vanished. Anansi was getting more impressive by the minute.

Osebo launched himself at Anansi, who sat in his chair, smiling. Before Osebo made contact, Anansi seemed to dissolve into nothingness. Osebo slammed into the empty chair, then whirled around.

Anansi — the real Anansi — suddenly reappeared

and whacked Osebo with his staff, sending him hurtling against another row of seats. Osebo got up, turned around, and glared at Anansi.

"Perhaps today I have a trick of my own," he said. He took out a walkie-talkie from his vest pocket and spoke into it. "Destroy the train!"

The train whistle shrieked in reply. In the next instant, the train lurched violently to one side. Sharon and Dr. Anokye looked out the window.

"We've switched to a side track!" Dr. Anokye cried.

Virgil tensed. Osebo wasn't alone. He had help — and they were trying to destroy the train! Static electricity tingled from his fingers. If only he didn't have to keep his Static identity a secret! Then he could help Anansi.

"We're going to crash!" Sharon screamed.

"No, we will not," Anansi said calmly.

Anansi jumped up and lifted himself through the hole in the roof that Osebo had created. Virgil rushed to the other side of the train and stuck his head out of the window so he could see what Anansi was up to. Just as he had guessed, three men wearing leopard makeup on their faces stood on top of the train. Osebo's men rushed toward Anansi. He avoided them by climbing down the side of the train, crawling along it like a spider over a wall. Virgil had never seen anything like it.

Then Virgil heard Dr. Anokye cry out. "No! Please!"

Virgil spun around. Osebo was pulling the briefcase away from the professor. Virgil's dad stepped up and tried to pry away the case.

"Like my son said, leave him alone!" said Mr. Hawkins.

Osebo growled and pushed Mr. Hawkins aside. Virgil raced back across the train car, but Sharon got to Osebo first and angrily stomped on his tail.

Osebo turned around and growled at Sharon. She smiled weakly. "My bad."

The leopard man yanked his tail out from under Sharon's foot, sending her tumbling.

Virgil grabbed a suitcase from the overhead rack and threw it at Osebo. The blow knocked him off of his feet.

"Stay away from my family!" Virgil yelled.

Osebo leaped up, but before he could charge at Virgil, the train lurched again.

"I should punish you for that," Osebo said, grabbing the briefcase, which had fallen to the floor. "But I'm out of time. And so are you!"

Suddenly, Virgil thought of a way to help. He reached into his pocket and pulled out a small metal gadget shaped like a ring with a line through it. He quickly zapped it with a small charge. It was a tracer. Osebo might get away, but Virgil would make sure that Anansi could find him again. As Osebo climbed out through the roof, Virgil tossed the tracer onto his back. It latched on.

Virgil looked out the window and watched as Osebo climbed into a hovering helicopter. Up ahead, he could see a large barricade at the end of the train track. Osebo was getting away — and they were trapped on a runaway train!

Everyone on the train car rushed to the front to see what was happening. Virgil held back. There might be another way he could help.

A squealing sound filled the air as the train's

brakes tried to bring it to a stop. Virgil knew Anansi must have taken control of the train. Was he too late?

The train slowed down, but it was going too fast to stop now, and the barricade was getting closer and closer.

"We're heading toward a cliff!" someone screamed.

Everyone was looking out the front of the train. Virgil knew his chance had come. He sent a powerful electromagnetic charge through the floor of the train, zapping the wheels to slow them down. The train creaked, groaned — and stopped just inches from the blockade!

Virgil sank into the nearest seat, exhausted. His father walked back and put a hand on his shoulder. "See, I told you Africa would be exciting."

Virgil got to his feet. He had to find Anansi and tell him about the tracer. Then he heard the happy shouts of the train passengers calling out Anansi's name. People lined the windows, calling out and waving. Virgil found an open spot and squeezed in.

Anansi was standing outside the train, smiling

and waving back. "Forgive me for not staying, but the leopard's trail grows cold," he said.

"Anansi! Wait!" Virgil yelled, but his voice was drowned out by the cheers of the other passengers. He watched as Anansi turned and walked away. And then, mysteriously, Anansi seemed to vanish into thin air.

CHAPTER TEN
Can You Keep a Secret?

It took a while for things to settle down. Buses came and transported the train passengers to a nearby village. Mr. Hawkins got the family settled into a hotel. Then they headed out to the local marketplace.

Wood stalls shaded vendors from the sun. They contained everything from fruits and vegetables to colored cloth and handmade pottery. Sharon started shopping right away. The first chance Virgil got, he found a quiet place and contacted Richie with the ShockVox. He explained what had happened on the train.

"And before I could tell him anything, he disappeared," Virgil finished.

"Well, you'd better do something," Richie replied. "The tracer's going to go dead in a few hours."

"I know, but I'm stuck in this village with my family until the train is fixed," Virgil said. Then, from the corner of his eye, he saw Sharon heading toward him. She was loaded down with bulging shopping bags. "Uh-oh. Gotta go. Ms. 'Shop-a-Zulu' is coming."

Virgil quickly pocketed the ShockVox and turned to face his sister. "Shouldn't you be pacing yourself on the shopping thing?"

"This is not a shopping 'thing,'" Sharon said defensively. "I'm exploring my African roots."

Then Sharon saw something from the corner of her eye. "Ooh, kente cloth!" she squealed, heading away.

Virgil sighed. He didn't know what to do. Then, across the street, he saw Dr. Anokye sitting at a table at an outdoor cafe. The professor might know something that could help him track down Anansi or Osebo.

Virgil approached the table. Dr. Anokye was eating a plate of what looked like orange mush.

"Virgil!" the professor said, smiling. "Please sit down and join me. Would you like some *fufu*? My treat."

"Uh, looks good, but I'll pass," Virgil said, sitting down. "I just wanted to ask you — what did Osebo take from you?"

"A map of ancient Kumasi, home of the great Ashanti nation," Dr. Anokye replied. "I believe I've found the location of a lost palace."

Virgil was surprised. "A palace? In Ghana?"

The doctor nodded. "Oh, yes. The Ashanti were talented goldsmiths. The palace might have artifacts worth millions, if it were accessible."

"What do you mean?" Virgil asked.

"According to the maps, it lies at the bottom of the largest man-made lake in the world — Lake Volta," Dr. Anokye explained.

"A lake won't stop Osebo."

The voice came from behind them. Virgil turned to see a dark shadow slide toward them. The shadow transformed into Anansi.

"I regret that I have lost Osebo's trail, doctor," Anansi said. "I fear I have no way to find him."

"Actually, you do," Virgil said. He stood up and leaned toward Anansi, whispering. "Can you keep a secret?"

Anansi and Virgil left Dr. Anokye and went to Virgil's hotel room. Virgil took the tracer from his pocket and showed it to Anansi.

"It's a tracer," Virgil said. "My friend Richie makes them, but I'm the only one who can track them."

"And why is that?"

Virgil grinned and raised his hands. Static electricity poured out of them, creating a charge around his entire body.

Anansi looked shocked. "How did you . . . ?"

"I'm a super hero, too," Virgil said. "Don't tell my dad."

Anansi smiled. "Then you are going to have to help me."

"Yeah, but what do I say to my pops?" Virgil wondered. "Excuse me, Father, but I'm going to save the ancient treasure of the Ashanti! Don't wait up!"

Suddenly, the sound of footsteps approached the door, followed by the jingling of keys.

"Uh-oh . . . that's him!" Virgil cried.

Anansi placed a hand on Virgil's shoulder. "Do not move."

In the next instant, Virgil and Anansi seemed to vanish from view. An illusion appeared in one of the beds in the hotel room. It looked like Virgil — fast asleep under the covers.

The door opened, and Mr. Hawkins and Sharon stepped in.

"Hey, Virgil, hungry?" Mr. Hawkins asked.

"We actually found a Burger Fool!" Sharon chimed in. Then they noticed Virgil sleeping.

"He must be exhausted," Mr. Hawkins whispered. "Let him sleep." Then he and Sharon quietly backed up and closed the door.

Anansi and Virgil became visible once more. Virgil walked over and looked at the illusion of himself, asleep. It seemed so real!

"People see what I want them to see," Anansi

said. "When your family comes back, they'll see you still here."

"You have to teach me how to do that!" Virgil said, impressed.

"Not now," Anansi said gravely. "We must find Osebo."

CHAPTER ELEVEN
A Real Cliff-hanger

Virgil quickly changed into his Static gear. He charged up his flying disk and soared out the window. To his surprise, Anansi put his feet on the *bottom* of the disk and hung upside-down, his arms folded calmly.

"How can you do that?" Static asked. It was like Anansi had superglue on the bottom of his shoes or something.

"Stick-to-itiveness," Anansi replied from below.

Static followed the tracer, which let out tiny

beeping sounds as it led them to Osebo. They flew over villages and plains.

"We are heading toward Kumasi," Anansi said. "Osebo must be after the treasure already."

Suddenly, the tracer went dead. "Dang!" Static exclaimed. "I lost it! The tracer must be out of juice."

"Not to worry. I see them!" Anansi called out.

Static looked down at a construction site below. Trailers and small buildings had been set up next to a wide gorge with a deep, deep drop.

Static lowered the flying disk. As he got closer, he could see Osebo standing in front of one of the buildings. His men, their faces painted to look like leopards, carried crates marked TNT — dynamite.

Before they reached the ground, Anansi did a somersault off the flying disk and landed on his feet. Static hovered next to him, low to the ground. Osebo looked up in shock.

"Is he another of your illusions, spider?" Osebo asked.

"His name is Static," Anansi replied. "He's an American. You know how flashy they can be."

Osebo grinned. "As flashy as this?"

Without warning, the leopard man tossed a bundle of lit dynamite at Static and Anansi. The dynamite landed in front of Static.

"Look out!" Anansi yelled. He leaped up, knocking Static out of the way.

KABOOM! The dynamite exploded, sending the two heroes tumbling over the cliff. A shower of heavy rocks fell on top of them.

Osebo and his men looked over the gorge. There was no sign of life — just a steaming pile of rocks at the bottom of the gorge.

Osebo smiled smugly. "At last, the spider has been stepped on!"

He tossed a rock down onto the pile of rubble. Nothing moved, so Osebo walked away.

CHAPTER TWELVE
The Cat Is Caught

Suddenly, the pile of rocks begin to tremble. A bubble-shaped electric force field blasted through the rocks. Static and Anansi were crouched safely inside the bubble.

"That is a very useful ability," Anansi said, admiration in his voice.

"I practice on weekends," Static joked.

The bubble burst, and Static charged his flying disk again. Anansi latched onto the bottom and they flew to the top of the gorge.

Osebo and his men had gone — and from the looks of it, had taken the dynamite with them.

"They have escaped," Anansi said gravely, jumping down to the ground.

"Well, it's not like he can blow a hole in the bottom of the lake and let all of the water out, right?" Static asked.

Anansi's face looked troubled. "Lake Volta is formed by a dam," he explained. "If Osebo were to destroy it, the lake would pour into the valley —"

"— and he could find the hidden palace and the gold," Static finished.

Anansi nodded. "Yes. And destroy thousands of homes as well."

Anansi attached himself to the flying disk again and directed Static toward the Akosombo River Dam.

The waters of Lake Volta gleamed deep blue beneath the star-filled night sky. The huge dam spanned the width of the lake. Gigantic stone walls jutted up from the water. On one sloped wall, water poured from six huge pipes.

Static spotted a truck and one of Osebo's men standing next to an entrance leading inside the dam. The man's back was turned to them, and he was speaking into a walkie-talkie.

"Number Two, reporting in," the man said. "No sign of anyone yet."

Static lowered the flying disk. Anansi hung upside-down, right behind the man's back.

"And you call yourself a lookout," Anansi quipped.

The man turned, stunned. Anansi grabbed him underneath his shoulders and Static raised the flying disk. The man dropped the walkie-talkie as Anansi lifted him into the air, his legs dangling below him. Static flew across the dam and hovered over the lake.

"Where is Osebo?" Anansi demanded.

"Inside the dam, with the others," said the panicked henchman.

"Where in the dam?" Anansi asked.

"The bottom tunnel!"

Anansi glanced up at Static. "He has been most helpful. What should his reward be?"

Static grinned. "How about we take him for a spin?"

Static began to rotate the disk, flipping them around and around. Finally, he stopped abruptly, sending Osebo's henchman flying through the air. He landed in the lake with a splash and came up sputtering.

Static and Anansi flew to the dam entrance and raced down a long flight of stairs. Ahead, they saw a long tunnel dug into the base of the dam. It looked like it had been carved out of solid stone. Osebo's voice rang out from inside the tunnel.

"Tonight we celebrate!" he said confidently. "We bury the spider! We dig up the gold!"

Static and Anansi crept closer, spying on Osebo. His men were attaching the bundles of dynamite to the sides of the tunnel wall.

"He seems so happy," Anansi whispered. "It's a shame to disappoint him."

Static examined the tunnel. Round lamps hung down from the ceiling. That gave him an idea.

"Shield your eyes," he told Anansi.

Anansi obeyed, and Static zapped the lamps with a supercharged blast of electric energy. Hot, white light exploded from the lamps, blinding

Osebo and his henchmen. They cried out in pain, covering their eyes.

Anansi entered the tunnel. One by one, he knocked down the henchmen with his staff. When the lights finally died out, not a single man was left standing. But Osebo was gone.

"Where did Whiskers go?" Static asked.

Just then, the sound of footsteps echoed from the other end of the tunnel. Anansi motioned toward the fallen henchmen. "See to them," he told Static. Then he ran after Osebo.

Static zapped the henchmen with a static charge, trapping them flat against the walls of the tunnel.

Outside the tunnel, Anansi faced Osebo. The leopard man stood on top of the dam.

"Osebo!" Anansi called out. "The game is finished!"

As Anansi spoke, another Anansi — an illusion — appeared on the other side of Osebo.

"There are no moves for you to make," he said, and a third Anansi appeared.

Osebo spun in a circle, a look of anger forming on his face.

"The spider weaves his web," Anansi said finally, as a fourth became visible. All four Anansis surrounded Osebo, drawing closer. They smiled.

"And now, the cat is caught."

Osebo held up his right claw. In it, he grasped a remote control device.

"But a cat has many lives, Anansi," Osebo said. "I can still detonate the explosives with this! Unless you want your flying friend crushed, you will reveal yourself."

"You press the button and we all go," Anansi pointed out.

But Osebo didn't waver. "Do not tempt me," he said.

Anansi knew Osebo was dangerous enough to carry out his threat. One by one the Anansi illusions vanished until only the real Anansi was left.

Osebo smiled . . . but the smile disappeared as an electric charge zapped the remote, sending it flying out of his hand. He turned to see Static at the tunnel entrance.

"You guys play 'Keep Away' over here?" he cracked.

Osebo growled. In a flash, he pulled an iron

claw from his costume and threw it at Static. The claw snagged against Static's cape, throwing him against the wall. The remote control flew out of his hand.

Before Osebo could catch it, Anansi flipped in the air and snatched it away. He landed on his feet just as Osebo swiped at him with his metal claw, knocking the staff out of Anansi's hands. He swiped again, tearing the front of Anansi's costume. The attacks forced Anansi back, until he was standing with his back to the top of the high wall of the dam.

"At the very least, I will finally be rid of you," Osebo growled, and he leaped through the air — his arms and legs wide, ready to push Anansi over the edge.

But Anansi stepped backward over the dam, his feet sticking to the side of the wall — thanks to his spiderlike powers. Osebo flew right over Anansi, and over the edge of the wall! Static rushed to the edge and looked down to see Osebo groaning on the concrete below.

"And they say cats always land on their feet!" Static joked.

CHAPTER THIRTEEN
Role Models

Anansi and Static took Osebo to the authorities, and Virgil and his family were able to enjoy the rest of their trip without any other villains getting involved. Virgil saw amazing people, places, and animals, but nothing compared to fighting alongside Anansi.

They spent the last day of the trip back in Accra, the capital. Virgil was packing his suitcase when his dad walked in, carrying a newspaper.

"Hey, I just read that the government is going to start an underwater expedition to find the Ashanti

Palace now that Dr. Anokye has the map back," Mr. Hawkins announced.

"Cool," Virgil said. It felt good knowing he had had something to do with how things worked out.

Mr. Hawkins checked his watch. "I'd better go down to the front desk and check us out. Don't take too long, Virgil."

Virgil nodded and turned back to his suitcase. Then he heard a voice behind him.

"I will miss you, my friend." Virgil turned as Anansi dropped, headfirst, from the ceiling and landed upright. "I will miss your good humor, too," Anansi added. He held out his hand, and Virgil shook it.

"I'll miss you, too, Anansi," Virgil said. "I never knew how important it would be to meet a role model like you."

"Role model?" Anansi asked.

Virgil nodded. Soul Power was a great role model, but he was retired. Kids didn't know who he was anymore. But Anansi was out there making the world a better place. People loved him. Somehow, it felt good knowing that.

"Yeah, a black super hero," Virgil said. "I don't know . . . it validates me somehow."

"Heroes come in every color, my friend," Anansi replied.

"I know," Static said. "It's just that sometimes I wish that there was a black super hero back home for folks to look up to. Someone like you."

Anansi smiled and placed a hand on Virgil's arm. "Oh, but there is," he said. "And he is my hero, too."

It didn't sink in right away, but then Virgil realized Anansi was talking about *him*. He blushed.

"Thanks," Virgil replied.

He was going to bring a lot of memories back home with him from Africa, but being called a hero by Anansi — that's a memory he knew he would never forget!

If you enjoyed *Static Shock: Soul Power* make sure to check out the first book in the series . . .

DOUBLE TROUBLE

Meet Virgil Hawkins, a street-smart city kid with attitude. Well, he used to be, anyway — until he did some unexpected face-time with a chemical compound of mutagenic gas.

Now Virgil's a street-smart kid with attitude and super powers! His new extreme sport is gliding on magnetic trash can lids AND zapping bad dudes into submission.

Too bad none of this hero stuff helps with homework — or girls.